DISCARD

Dora's Picnic

by Christine Ricci
illustrated by Susan Hall

Ready-to-Read

Simon Spotlight/Nick Jr.

New York   London   Toronto   Sydney   Singapore

Based on the TV series *Dora the Explorer*® as seen on Nick Jr.®

SIMON SPOTLIGHT
An imprint of Simon & Schuster Children's Publishing Division
1230 Avenue of the Americas,
New York, New York 10020

22 24 26 28 30 29 27 25 23 21
0810 LAK
Ricci, Christine.
Dora's picnic / by Christine Ricci.
p. cm.—(Ready-to-read. Level 1, Dora the explorer ; 1)
Summary: Dora and her animal friends all contribute something to bring to
a picnic at Play Park. Features rebuses.
ISBN 0-689-85238-X
1. Rebuses. [1. Picnicking—Fiction. 2. Animals—Fiction. 3. Parks—Fiction. 4. Rebuses.]
I. Title. II. Series.
PZ7.R355 Do 2003
[E]—dc21
2002004518

Hi! I am  . We are going to a picnic at Play Park! Play Park has a ![slide], a ![sandbox], and ![swings].

DORA

SLIDE

SANDBOX

SWINGS

My **mami** is helping me make -and-

PEANUT-BUTTER   JELLY

sandwiches for the picnic.

 is my best friend.

BOOTS

He loves !

BANANAS

 **BOOTS** **has a bunch of** 🍌 **BANANAS**
for the picnic.

BENNY is riding his **BICYCLE** to the picnic.

He is carrying juice

APPLE

in his .

BASKET

Here comes the .

BIG RED CHICKEN

The has a big of

BIG RED CHICKEN   BAG

 for the picnic.

POPCORN

Yummy!

Look!  BABY BLUE BIRD has a bowl of fruit in her  WAGON.

What did  bring to the picnic?

TICO

 TICO brought BREAD .

The BREAD is filled with

BLUEBERRIES and NUTS !

ISA made **CUPCAKES** to share
with everyone.

I like chocolate  CUPCAKES

with PINK icing. What kind

do you like?

Look out for .
SWIPER
He will try to swipe
the food we brought.

 is hiding behind
the .
Say, "Swiper, no swiping!"
Yay! You stopped !

We made it to Play Park!
This  is perfect for
TABLE
our picnic. But first we
want to play!

likes to go down

the **.**

BABY BLUE BIRD is making a **SAND CASTLE**

in the .

SANDBOX

The pushes

BIG RED CHICKEN   **BOOTS**

and on the AUA.

ISA   **SWINGS**

This is the best picnic!
We can all share the food.
What would **you** bring
to a picnic?